Big Book of Bears

includes:

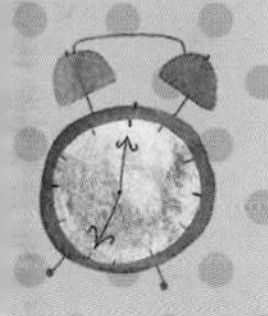

I can't **BEAR** it!

Always There Bear

Little Bear's Big Adventure

Baby Bear and the Big, Wide World

The Bear who loved to Dance

by

Monika Filipina Trzpil

Bears
dance
TAP
BIG BOOK
BIG BOOK OF DANCE
encyclopedia
Sketch book
BIGGER BOOK
Ballet
BOOK
How to Dance
ROCK
JAZZ
NEW
DANCE

Bear loved to dance.

He practised
in his bedroom
every day.

Bear wanted to
dance with the other
animals, but he was
very clumsy.

Bear tried ballet.
But all the giraffes just
laughed at him.

Thud!
Thud!
Stomp!
'You're not graceful enough for ballet,' they mocked.

So Bear tried breakdance.

But the monkeys simply giggled ...

'You're not bendy enough for breakdance,' they sniggered.

Bear tried tap dance too.

But the rhinos grumbled at Bear.

'You're not quick enough for tap dance!' they scoffed.

Tap ... Tap ... Tap ...
Tap ...
Tap ...
Whack!

Then Bear tried swing ...

... but Zebra wasn't happy.

'You're too strong for swing!' she cried.

Bear even tried

synchronized swimming ...

But the tortoises laughed at Bear too.

Splash ...
Splash...
Splash...
Splash ...
Splash...
Splosh!
Splash...
Splash ...

Poor Bear couldn't seem to do anything right …

Until one day he noticed a poster ...

first ever

ICE SKaTING

COMPETITION

- for bears only -

JOIN NOW:

Pond in the Woods
12 Oaks Street

Bear decided to take part in the competition.

When the day came he was very nervous.

But Bear ...

was ...

simply ...

amazing!

The judges loved Bear's dancing.
'10 out of 10!' they cheered.

Bear won first place in the competition
and he was given a shiny gold medal.

1
2
3

And all the other animals ...

learnt that dancing on ice ...

was not easy ...

at all!

I can't BEAR it!

Written by Carrie Hennon
Illustrated by Barbara Bakos

This is

She might look like a sweet little girl …

… but sometimes she can be a real
GRUMP!

This is

Bear.

When Clare doesn’t want to do something she yells,

‘I can’t BEAR it!’

That’s when Bear steps in.

'BEEP! BEEP! BEEP!' went the alarm.
It was time to get ready for school.

'I can't BEAR it!' groaned Clare.
'I'd rather stay in bed.'

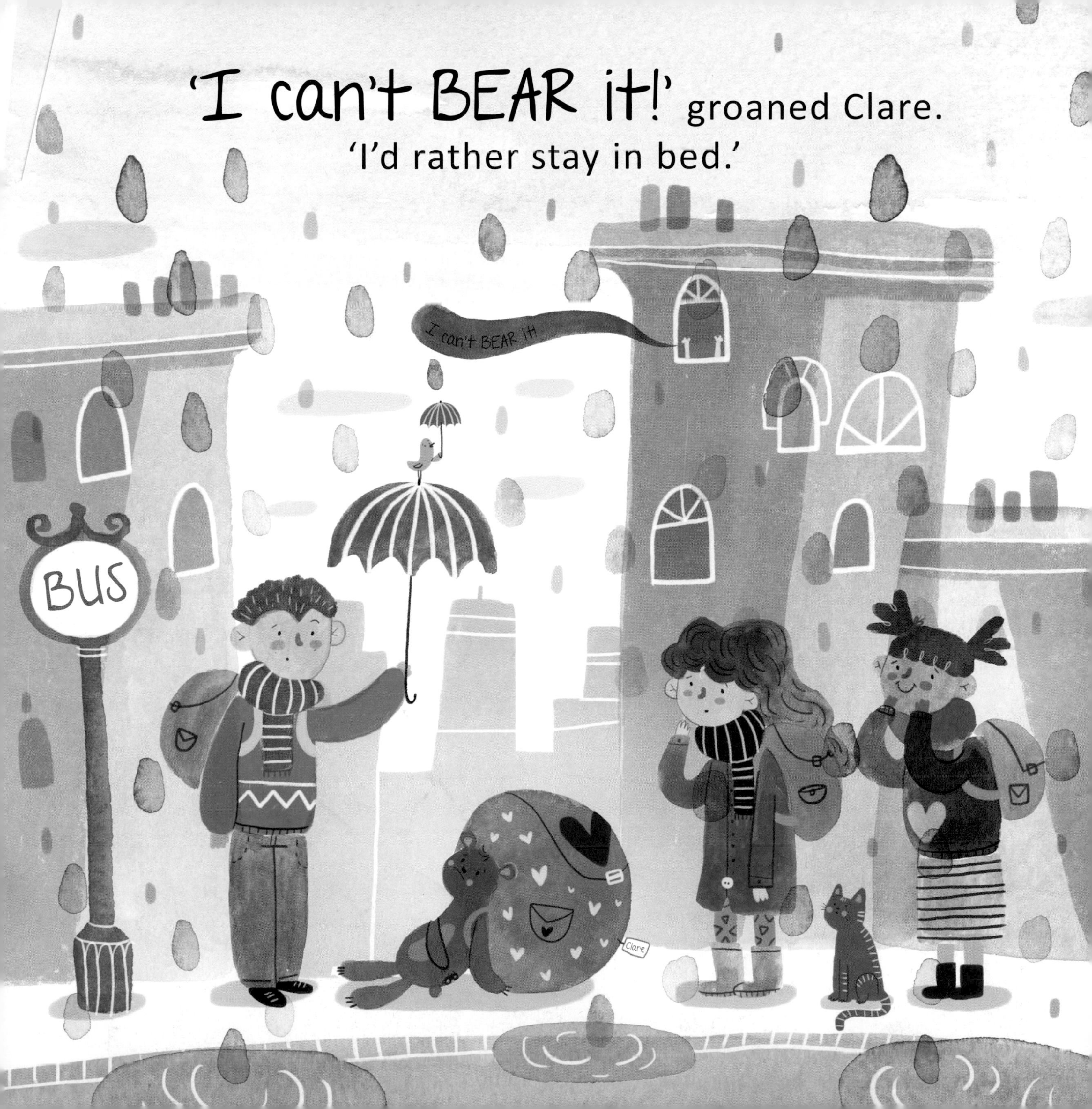

'First position please girls,'

said the ballet teacher, as the dance class began.

'I can't BEAR it!' complained Clare.
'I'd rather fly my kite.'

'Screech! Screech! SCREECH!'

went the violins in the music lesson.

‘I can’t BEAR it!’

yelled Clare.
‘I’d rather listen to my own kind of music.’

‘Lunch is ready!’

called Dad,
as he put a bowl of crunchy green salad on the table.

'I can't BEAR it!' moaned Clare.
'I'd rather eat a big slice of pizza.'

'On your marks,
get set, GO!'

started the three-legged
race on sports day.

'I can't BEAR it!'
huffed Clare.

'I'd rather hang
upside down
from a tree.'

When Mum asked Clare to tidy her room,
all Clare heard was, 'Blah, blah, blah!'

'I can't BEAR it!' sighed Clare.

'I'd rather play video games.'

'Come on Clare, it's time to help with the washing up,' called Mum.

'I can't BEAR it!'

grumbled Clare.

'I'd rather watch cartoons.'

'Come and give me a kiss, dear,'
said Grandma, as she puckered her lips …

'I can't BEAR it!' shrieked Clare.
'I'd rather kiss the dog.'

And so things continued ...

Every time Clare didn't want to do something, poor Bear had to take her place.

'BEAR?!'

Until one day, Bear was nowhere to be found …

'I can't BEAR it!'

Always There Bear

Written by Trudi Granger
Illustrated by Gareth Llewhellin

Everyone needs a bear that's always there ...

A sunny, sandy seaside bear.

A much too wet to go outside bear.

A play-day with a friend at home bear.

A read a book alone bear.

A very happy birthday bear.

A sulky, grouchy, grumpy bear.

An in the car ... or bus
... or train bear.

A scoot ... or ride a trike ... or bike bear.

A full of bounce from toes to head bear.

A sore throat and snuffly nose in bed bear.

A playing together in the park bear.

A stay close, keep safe after dark bear.

An icy, snowy, all gone white bear.

A bright and blowy, fly a kite bear.

Everyone needs a bear that's always there ...

... An all day ... all night ... goodnight bear.

Little Lost Panda

Written by
Ellie Wharton

Illustrated by
Dubravka Kolanovic

Little Panda loved running ahead of Mummy Panda in the bamboo forest.

'Come back!'

Mummy Panda was always shouting.

One day, Little Panda ran further than he had ever done before. He ran so far that he lost the path, and although he waited and waited for Mummy Panda's call, it never came.

Little Panda was lost!

Little Panda sat down in a clearing
and rubbed his eyes with his furry paws.
He wanted Mummy Panda to be there
when he opened them. Instead,
a little bird was sitting on his shoulder.

'What's the matter, Little Panda?'
asked the little bird.

'I've lost my mummy and I'm all alone!'
sobbed Little Panda.

'Nonsense!' said the little bird.
'You're not alone, I'm here.
And I'm sure I saw something furry
with round ears up ahead.
It might be your mummy …

follow me!'

Little Panda followed the little
bird and before long they heard
a rustle of leaves.

Maybe it was Mummy Panda,
thought Little Panda excitedly.

The rustling stopped abruptly
and a furry head with round ears
poked up through the leaves.

But it wasn't Mummy Panda at all.
It was …

a bamboo rat!

'You're too small to be my mummy!' said Little Panda disappointedly.

'That's true,' said the bamboo rat, 'but I did see something bigger with a white face and dark patches around its eyes in the trees up ahead!'

Little Panda thanked the bamboo rat and they set off in the direction he was pointing.

Soon enough, Little Panda spotted something sitting in a tree with a white face and dark patches around its eyes. Little Panda climbed up the tree as fast as he could.

But it wasn't Mummy Panda at all, it was …

a flying red

and white squirrel!

'You're too small and too fast to be my mummy!'
said Little Panda disappointedly.

'I am,' said the flying squirrel,
'but I did see something sitting
quite still by the waterfall up ahead
and it was bigger and furrier too!'

Little Panda thanked the flying squirrel
and they set off in the direction he was pointing.

Very soon Little Panda reached the waterfall, and sure enough, sitting quite still beside it was something big and furry.

But it wasn't Mummy Panda at all, it was …

a golden

snub-nosed monkey!

'You're too golden to be my mummy!'
said Little Panda disappointedly.

'Yes I am,' said the monkey,
'but I did happen to see something black and white and furry
not too far up ahead, at the top of that mountain.'

Little Panda thanked the monkey and they set off
in the direction he was pointing.

Little Panda began to climb the small mountain
and before long he came face to face with
something black and white and furry …

But it wasn't Mummy Panda at all, it was …

a snow leopard!

'Quick,
run or he'll eat you!'

shouted the little bird to Little Panda.

Little Panda didn't wait to find out what the snow leopard had to say. He turned and he ran and he ran and he ran until he was completely out of breath.

Little Panda found himself back in the clearing.

'I'll NEVER find Mummy,' he said miserably
to the little bird. 'I'm all alone!'

'Not ENTIRELY alone,'
said a voice in the trees.

Little Panda looked up and saw two
furry ears poking out from a tree up ahead.
Was it … could it be?

But it wasn't Mummy Panda at all,
it was …

. . . a red panda!

'You're NOT Mummy Panda!' said Little Panda,
with tears welling up in his eyes.

'Don't cry,' said the red panda,
coming to sit beside Little Panda.

'Follow me, I know just where she'll be.'

Soon they found the path that Little Panda
had lost and Little Panda heard a familiar voice.

'Come back!' it shouted.

Little Panda ran and he ran and he ran,
straight into the big furry bear hug of Mummy Panda.

'There you are, Little Panda!'
Mummy Panda exclaimed happily.
'You must promise never to run off again.
The forest is a dangerous place for a little lost panda!'

Little Panda nodded. 'I promise!' he said,
thankful to be back in his mummy's arms.

Then Little Panda remembered
the little bird and the red panda
and how kind they had been to him
when he thought he was all alone.

'Mummy Panda?
Can my new friends have a bear hug too?'

'Of course!' said Mummy Panda,
gathering Little Panda and his new friends
into her furry beary arms.

The End

Little Bear's Big Adventure

Written by Julia Hubery
Illustrated by Gill Guile

'What shall we do today,
Little Bear?' asked Mother Bear.

Little Bear peeked out of their
shady cave at the hot sun.
'Can we stay here, where it's lovely
and cool?' he asked.

'If we do that, we will have
nothing to eat,' said Mother Bear.
'But I have an idea. Shall we go
somewhere as cool as a cave,
where there's lots of food
we can catch and pick?'

Little Bear jumped up and down.
'Where is it? What will we catch?
What will we pick?' he asked.

'It's a surprise,' laughed Mother
Bear, 'but here's a clue. What is
your favourite pudding?'

'Strawberries?!!'

Little Bear shouted.

'YUM, let's go!'

At first Little Bear skipped along happily, but as the day grew hotter, he grew **tired** and **grumpy.**

'This isn't very cool!' complained Little Bear, as Mother Bear stopped on a high, rocky ledge in the sun.

'Hush, come and look – here's your surprise,' said Mother Bear.

Little Bear climbed up beside her, and looked down. Shining out of the forest, like a silver moon in a deep green sky, was a beautiful, cool pool.

'Hurray!' yelled Little Bear.

They followed a stream which
bubbled from the rocks,
splashing into rainbows
as it tumbled **down ...**

down ...

down ...

… and into the pool.

The water was icy-fresh and
delicious, and Little Bear **loved** it.

'First we'll have a little rest,' said Mother Bear, 'then I'll teach you to fish, and we'll pick our strawberries, and soon …'

'... We'll have a perfect picnic!' shouted Little Bear. Little Bear snuggled up with Mother Bear in the mossy shade, but he was too excited to nap. 'I will surprise Mummy,' he thought,

'I'll make the perfect picnic myself!'

'Strawberries first,' he said, for he knew the little nooks where wild strawberries love to grow. When he had enough for two hungry bears, he arranged them carefully on a leaf. 'Now, I must catch fish,' said Little Bear.

Little Bear stretched his paw down into the stream, and as he did, he saw a reflection in the water!

Something **huge ...**

and **dark ...**

and **HUNGRY ...**

was reaching out
to **GRAB** him!

SPLASH!

Little Bear lost his balance,
and toppled into the pool.

Down …

down …

down …

he sank.

The huge dark
creature jumped in after him!

Little Bear struggled
to escape, but strong
hairy arms grabbed at him,
caught him, held him tight
and pulled him from the pool.

Little Bear wriggled
free and saw …

… Mother Bear!

'Mummy!' he cried. 'Where is the B-big H-hairy Sc-scary **Thing** that grabbed me?!!'

'I am the Big Hairy Scary **Thing!'** she laughed.

'I only wanted to make you a wake-up surprise,' said Little Bear.

'That was a kind idea,' smiled Mother Bear, 'but surprises are tricky. You must be careful, or nasty surprises get mixed up with the nice ones!'

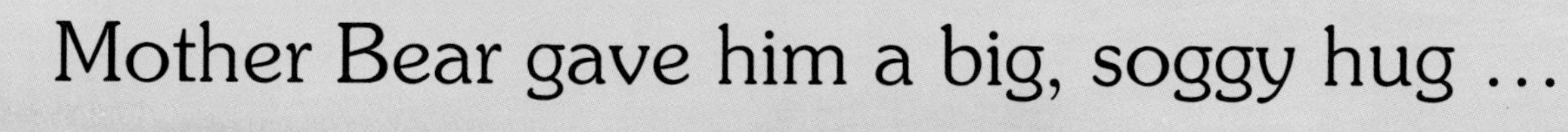

Mother Bear gave him a big, soggy hug …

… and found there was one
more surprise for them both!

Baby Bear

and the Big, Wide World

Written by Ellie Patterson
Illustrated by Dubravka Kolanovic

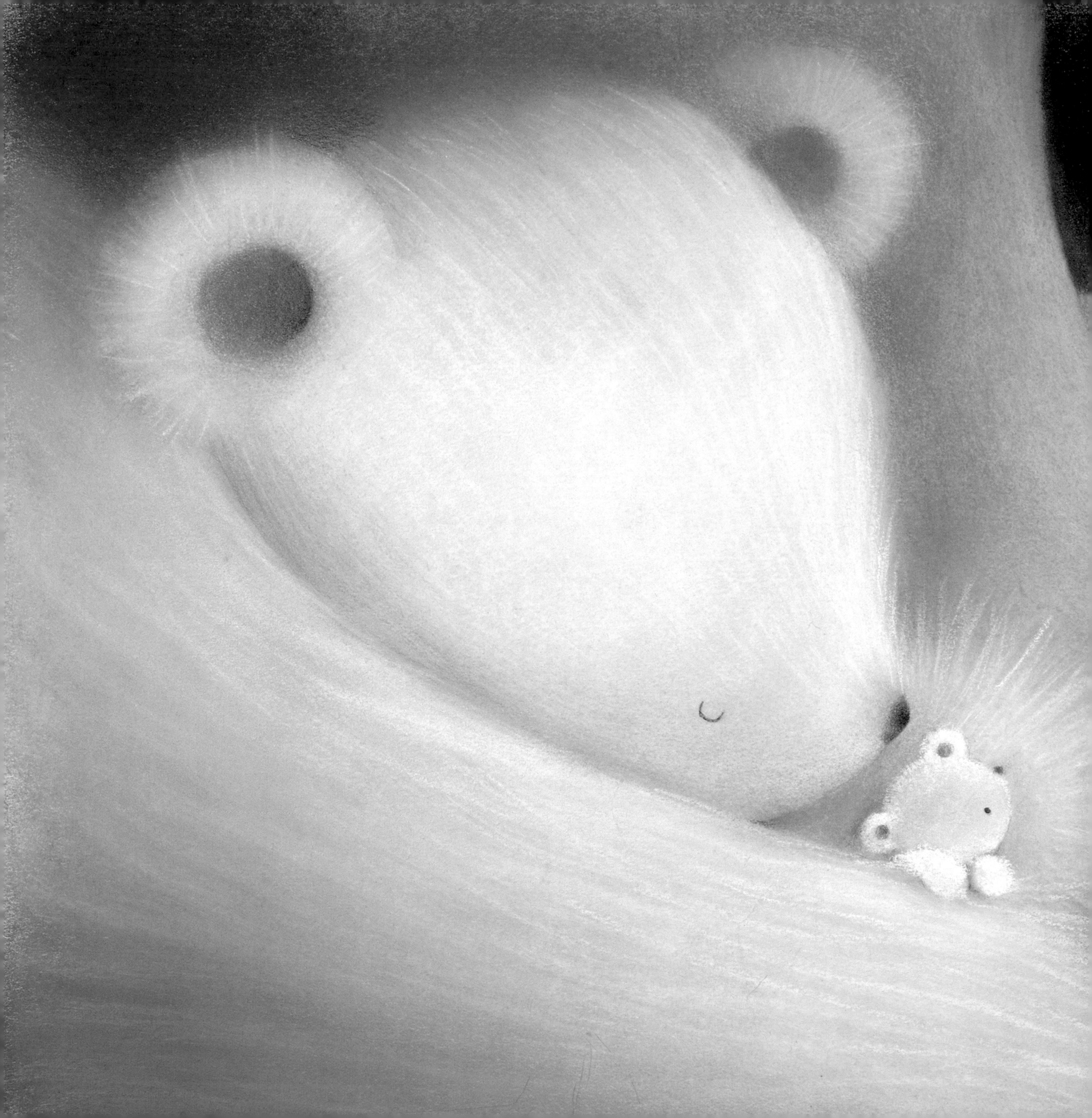

Inside his cosy den, Baby Bear was snug and warm in Mummy Bear's arms. Outside, the big, wide world was cold and white.

No matter how hard he tried,
Baby Bear could not sleep. He was curious.
Slipping out from Mummy Bear's arms, Baby Bear
peeped out at the big, wide world. It looked a
little frightening, but he wanted to explore.

Stepping outside, Baby Bear saw that there were footprints. Big footprints. Huge footprints! A little scared, he decided to follow them to see where they led.

The big footprints went on and on, winding down a path and through deep, dark woods. Baby Bear looked up at the sky and thought that it looked like a big, black blanket. Then he saw the moon and thought that it looked like a big hole in the big, black blanket.

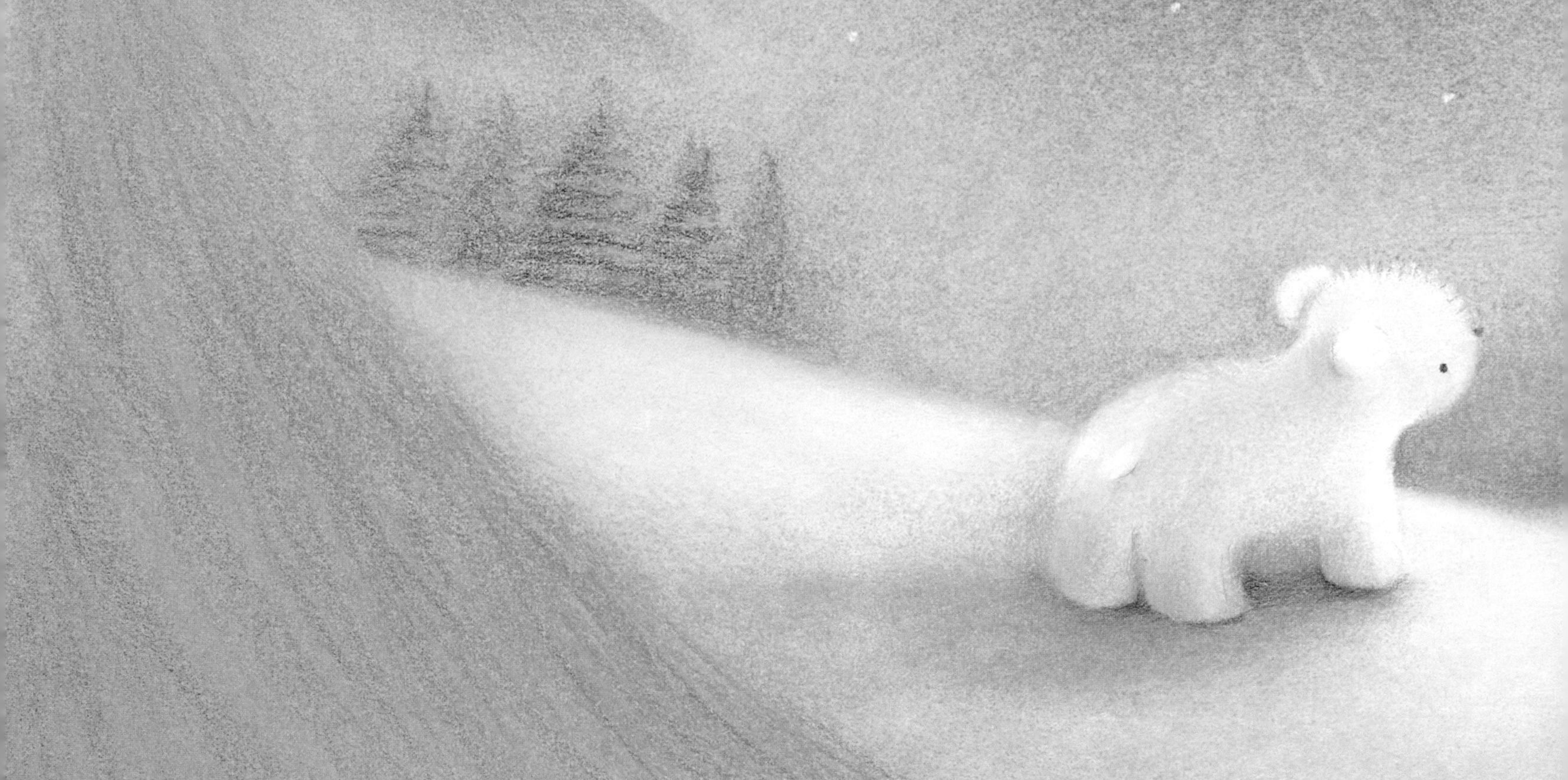

Suddenly, Baby Bear began to feel very small and very alone.

Soon, Baby Bear came to the ocean.
It was so big and so wide that just looking
at it made Baby Bear feel even smaller.

Baby Bear sat down and began to wish that he
hadn't left Mummy Bear's snug, warm arms.

Suddenly there was a splash, then there was a sniffle, and then a small creature flopped onto the rock beside Baby Bear.

'Who are you?' asked the small creature, looking curiously at Baby Bear.

'I'm Baby Bear,' said Baby Bear.
'Who are you?'

'I'm Sammy Seal,'
said Sammy Seal.

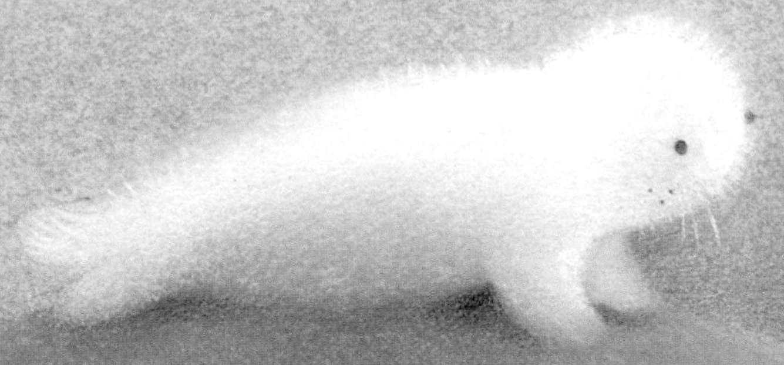

‘Are you scared of the big, wide world too?’ asked Baby Bear, realising that Sammy Seal must find it even scarier than he did because he was so small.

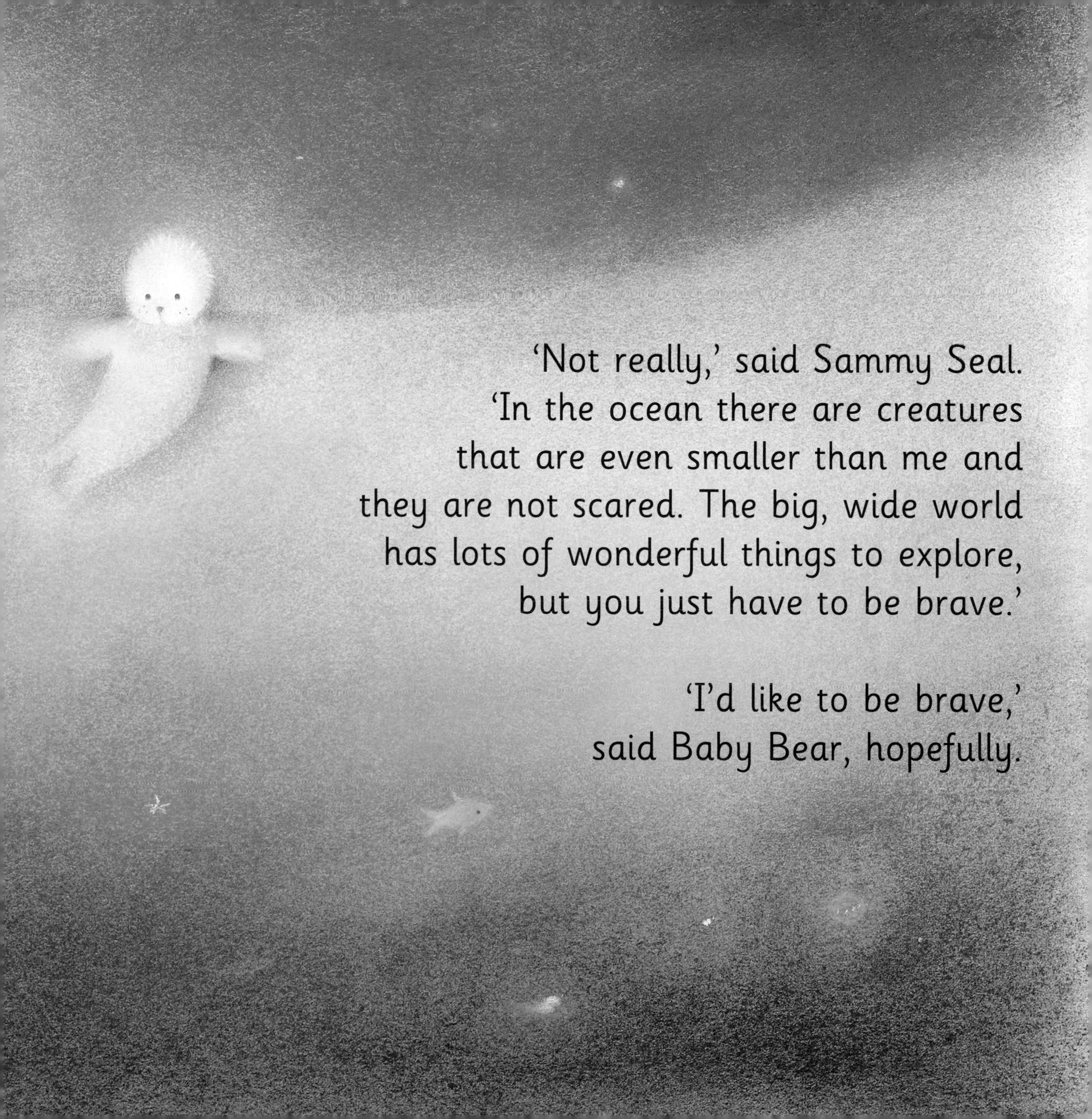

'Not really,' said Sammy Seal.
'In the ocean there are creatures
that are even smaller than me and
they are not scared. The big, wide world
has lots of wonderful things to explore,
but you just have to be brave.'

'I'd like to be brave,'
said Baby Bear, hopefully.

‘Well, why don’t you come on a big adventure with me?’ Sammy Seal suggested. ‘I know lots of exciting things that we can do.’

‘OK!’ agreed Baby Bear, feeling brave all of a sudden.

From the top of a big iceberg in the middle of the big, blue ocean, Baby Bear and Sammy Seal watched whales flipping and somersaulting out of the water and named each of the stars in the sky.

Baby Bear began to feel very brave indeed sitting on top of the big iceberg with his new friend, Sammy Seal.

Soon the big sun began to rise over the big, blue ocean. The world was filled with light and seemed like a warm and welcoming place once more. But it was time to go home.

So Baby Bear and Sammy Seal swam back to the shore.

Baby Bear thanked Sammy Seal for
showing him that the big, wide world
wasn't as scary as he had first thought.
They agreed to meet up soon for
another big adventure.

Baby Bear followed the big footprints all the way home. He crept into Mummy Bear's arms as quietly as he could and fell soundly asleep, safe in the knowledge that the big, wide world is actually not that scary when you have a friend to share it with.